# Lizzie's Storm

To my mother, for always
making stories important
S.F

For Lauren and Rachel
M.W.

# Lizzie's Storm

## By Sally Fitz-Gibbon

with illustrations by Muriel Wood

Fitzhenry & Whiteside

Published in Canada by Fitzhenry & Whiteside,
195 Allstate Parkway, Markham, Ontario L3R 4T8

Published in the United States by Fitzhenry & Whiteside,
121 Harvard Avenue, Suite 2, Allston, Massachusetts 02134

www.fitzhenry.ca     godwit@fitzhenry.ca.

**National Library of Canada Cataloguing in Publication Data**
Fitz-Gibbon, Sally, 1949-
Lizzie's storm / by Sally Fitz-Gibbon ; with illustrations by Muriel Wood
(New beginnings)
ISBN 1-55041-793-2 (bound).—ISBN 1-55041-795-9 (pbk.)
1. Depressions—1929—Prairie—Juvenile fiction.
2. Immigrant children—Prairie—Juvenile fiction.
3. Prairie Provinces—History—1905-1945—Juvenile fiction.
I. Wood, Muriel  II. Title.  III. Series: New beginnings (Markham, Ont.)
PS8561.I87L59 2003     jC813'.54     C2002-905298-X
PZ7

**U.S. Publisher Cataloging-in-Publication Data**
(Library of Congress Standards)

Fitz-Gibbon, Sally.
Lizzie's storm : new beginnings / by Sally Fitz-Gibbon ; with illustrations by Muriel Wood. — 1st ed.
[64] p. : col. ill. ;  cm.  (New Beginnings)    Includes index.
Summary: When an accident leaves her orphaned, Lizzie's life in the bustling city of London is over forever. And nothing she has ever experienced could prepare her for her new home, a whole continent away on a dusty prairie farm in Canada.
ISBN 1-55041-793-2
ISBN 1-55041-795-9 (pbk.)
1. Orphans — Juvenile fiction.  2. Families — Juvenile fiction.  3. Depressions — 1929 —The Prairies — Juvenile fiction. (1. Orphans — Fiction.  2. Families — Fiction.  3. Depressions — 1929 — The Prairies — Fiction.)  I. Wood, Muriel .  II. Title.  III. Series.
[F]   21   2003

Fitzhenry & Whiteside acknowledges with thanks the Canada Council for the Arts, the Government of Canada through the Book Publishing Industry Development Program (BPIDP), and the Ontario Arts Council for their support for our publishing program.

Design by Wycliffe Smith Design Inc.

# Table of Contents

# Arrival: August, 1931

"Elizabeth. Elizabeth. What kind of fancy-dancey name is that? I can't get that out of my mouth every time I have to call you. Your name's Lizzie and that's it. Elizabeth, my foot!"

Lizzie's Uncle Bill towered over her. Stiffly he crossed his arms and stuck out his chin like a man waiting for an argument. Aunt Kate touched her husband's arm gently and frowned. She turned to Lizzie.

"Welcome to North Dakota. Welcome to Collinsville."

Lizzie stood open-mouthed, rooted to the station platform between her two cases and her new family. She listened to the wail of the departing train. It sounded like a child in pain. The tears that she'd held back for weeks began to sting her eyes and threaten to spill onto her cheeks. But she couldn't cry right away. She couldn't cry in front of her aunt and uncle. She hadn't even said hello.

Lizzie bent down to take hold of her suitcases and almost

collided with her aunt. Lizzie straightened up and looked into the woman's kind eyes.

"He...hello, Aunt Kate. I'm...I'm...," but Lizzie's tears defeated her and her lip wobbled as she tried to get out the last words.

"There there, child. After all you've been through this past month, you have every right to cry. Just you go ahead and let those tears fall." A rough hand patted Lizzie's arm. And two strong arms wrapped themselves around Lizzie's shaking shoulders and hugged tight. Lizzie let go and finally allowed her unhappiness to take over. All the terrible days after the accident—all those weeks of loneliness and despair—burst out. She howled.

"There, there. You've got us now. We'll look after you," whispered her aunt into Lizzie's ear.

"Sorry, Lizzie. Sorry for all your grief." Uncle Bill patted Lizzie's arm awkwardly. But his voice was kind.

LIZZIE WATCHED THE prairie roll past as she swayed on the wagon seat beside her aunt. She could feel Aunt Kate's protective arm around her. The breeze ruffled her hair. The horizon stretched farther than Lizzie had ever imagined possible.

"Aren't you lonely?" she whispered to her aunt.

Aunt Kate turned with a tired smile and nodded. "Sometimes. Yes, I am still lonely. But usually I'm too busy to be lonely...and too tired."

Lizzie watched the rumps of the horses moving up and down in front of the wagon.

"Don't you have a car?" she asked quietly.

"We do but we don't use it much. Horses are cheaper to feed than cars. It's 1931 and nobody has much work. There hasn't been rain to speak of for I don't know how long, and the fields are drying up and blowing away. So we don't have much money for extras right now, Lizzie. Gas is more of an extra than grass and hay."

The hard wooden seat made Lizzie restless. She ached from swaying and bumping over the ruts in the road. This trip seemed even longer than the journey by train. She stared around at the soft brown earth and the dry prairie grasses.

At last, far off in the distance stood a clump of trees. Lizzie put her hand above her eyes to cut out the glare. The road stretched ahead as straight as an arrow. The same trees gradually appeared bigger and bigger as they approached. But it took so long that Lizzie wanted to cry all over again.

"That's home, Lizzie," said Aunt Kate. "That's the farm. Seth and Robert are waiting to meet you. Robert is fourteen now, but Seth is a little closer to your age. He's twelve. They're a bit quiet but they're good boys. They help a lot on the farm. We all do. It's the only way to keep going now—have everybody do their bit."

The loneliness of the prairie pressed up against her. Lizzie felt something shrivel up inside. She wasn't sure she could get used to all the space. As the wind tugged at her hair and sprayed a fine mist of dust over her clothes, she thought about the neat lawns and gardens of home.

Home.

London, England. A long and scary train trip, then a whole week away by ship.

But England was no longer her home. Not since her parents had been killed in that terrible car accident and left her alone. Now it was just a place in her memory—full of echoing hallways and empty rooms.

# Chapter 2

# Not a Country Girl

The first morning, Lizzie took extra care to dress as simply as she could. She chose a school tunic, creased a little from her travel case but sturdy and plain. Then she tied up her hair into a ponytail. The only fancy touch to her outfit was the bright blue ribbon in her hair.

When Lizzie came down to breakfast, Seth was waiting.

"You're late, Lizzie. We have to go out and take care of the livestock before we eat. Come on. Robert's already gone to the barn." Seth motioned impatiently for Lizzie to follow. He was shorter than Robert but he was much bigger and stronger than Lizzie. He seemed huge beside her.

"No breakfast?" Lizzie's voice quivered.

Aunt Kate smiled. "That's right, Lizzie. Animals first, people second. That's how it is on a farm." She pointed to the corner by the door. "There's a pair of boots. You'll want them. And here's a kerchief. You'll need this if the wind picks up."

Puzzled, Lizzie took the kerchief from her aunt.

"For the dust, Lizzie. To keep the dust out of your nose and eyes if it starts to blow. Here. You tie it like this." Her aunt demonstrated how to fold and tie the square of material over Lizzie's face. "Now get yourself outside with Seth. He'll show you what to do."

THAT FIRST MORNING Lizzie decided she didn't like chickens.

She didn't like their smell. She didn't like their dust.

Most of all she didn't like their sharp beaks. She dropped the first egg when the mother hen turned around and pecked her hard on the back of her hand.

"Hey, Lizzie. You can't leave a broken egg on the floor. The hens get a taste for it, and then they start to eat their own eggs. You have to clean it up."

Lizzie eyed the broken shell and gooey mess at her feet. Nursing her sore hand, she stared up at her cousin.

"Now. You have to do it now before they find it. You'd better learn to deal with this because getting the eggs will be your job. It's easy and it'll give me time to get the pigs' water." Seth turned around and went out, leaving Lizzie to deal with the mess. He called back from the door, "And hurry up! I'll show you how to slop the pigs next."

LIZZIE AND PIGS weren't any better than Lizzie and chickens.

The pigs frightened Lizzie. They pushed up against the walls of the sty and squealed horribly when she and Seth picked up the buckets of watery food.

"It's so heavy," Lizzie grunted. Her bucket swung back and forth in her hands.

"Come on, Lizzie. You'll drop it." Seth glanced impatiently at Lizzie as he tipped the slop into the pigs' trough.

Hungry pig noises filled Lizzie's ears. Their smell filled her nose.

"I...I can't do it! I think I'm going to be sick!"

Lizzie's bucket swung back and forth one more time. Then it crashed to the ground, splashing her feet, her clothes—and her cousin.

"What did you do that for? You got slop all over me! Pa's going to skin you alive for wasting."

FEEDING AND MILKING the cows were no easier.

Robert called out to Lizzie and Seth from the barn door. He was taking full buckets of water off a flat, wooden sleigh-like thing harnessed to an enormous horse.

"Come on, you two. We've got to get this done before we send the cows outside." Robert looked down at Lizzie and her messy tunic. He smiled. "Having a little trouble? You'll soon get used to it." Then he turned, a heavy bucket held firmly in each hand. Sweat darkened Robert's shirtfront. The tendons in his arms bulged from the strain as the buckets swung, splashing water on the floor of the barn.

Lizzie was afraid of the slow-moving cattle. She wanted to stay as far away from them as she could. Gingerly she followed her cousins into the barn.

She hated the smell. She had to run outside and take deep breaths of fresh air to settle her stomach. When she returned, she leaned unhappily against the barn door.

The cousins stared at Lizzie.

"You can't milk from there, Lizzie," said Seth as he set a bucket under a black and white cow. "You have to get closer than that."

"At home I didn't have to work all the time."

"At home you didn't live on a farm. Here we all work." Robert looked at her over a forkful of hay. His voice was kinder than Seth's, and he smiled more than his brother.

"Tomorrow you can come out with us on the stoneboat

to get water from the slough. Then after lunch we'll go collect up the pats for drying. For fuel. For the stove." He laughed at his cousin's blank expression. "Don't you know about cowpats, Lizzie?"

Lizzie shook her head. She also didn't know about sloughs or stoneboats. She looked away, feeling stupid.

Robert took another forkful of hay and pitched it into the manger. The cows circled their long tongues around the dried grass and took it into their mouths. They chewed slowly and rhythmically. Lizzie watched, fascinated in spite of her fear.

"Tomorrow we'll explain all about cowpats and stone- boats, won't we, Seth?" Robert gave his brother a wink. Then he patted Lizzie on the shoulder before throwing another full load of hay into the manger.

# Stoneboats, Sloughs and Cowpats

"Come on, Lizzie. You're as slow as syrup in winter!" Lizzie rubbed her eyes and yawned. She remembered what her aunt had said about the boys—that they were quiet. Robert was a little quiet but Seth certainly wasn't. If he wasn't calling her names and laughing at her, he was telling her to do things she knew nothing about. Now he was slapping his hands on the table and telling her to get a move on.

"What Seth is trying to say to you, Kate, is that today is an extra special day. You have to get the chores done and then go out to the slough. The work today will be different from the daily chores." Aunt Kate made a shooing gesture with her hands at Seth. "And you can go out and get started and quit pestering Lizzie! Now get on with you."

Lizzie went back upstairs and looked through her clothes. Her pretty dresses were beginning to look grubby. Already the ever-present dust had sifted through everything. She touched one graying dress after the other. Then she found her old school uniform and put that on. After tying up her hair, she clattered down the stairs and out the back door.

ROBERT WAS WAITING with the odd sleigh-thing harnessed to the enormous horse.

He patted the creature's shoulder as Lizzie came up. "Meet Prince, the best dray horse this side of the state line."

Lizzie stepped back away from the huge beast. She hesitated before coming toward her cousin.

"It's all right. He's gentle. You could sit on him if you wanted."

"No thanks," whispered Lizzie, careful to stay out of reach of the horse's mouth. "What's that?" She pointed to the thing harnessed behind Prince.

"It's called a stoneboat," said Robert. "When the rain comes and the roads turn to gumbo, you can't get anything on wheels through the mud. So we use this thing instead. It has runners and it can go over almost everything."

"Ready, Lizzie? Ready to learn about sloughs and cowpats?" Seth grinned.

Lizzie had an awful feeling that it wasn't going to be much fun doing whatever they had planned for her.

Sloughs proved to be shallow ditches that ran beside the fields. They were regular with straight banks like they'd been measured.

"These were all dug by Pa and his father when they homesteaded here. Gramps was a sod-buster. He did most of the work by hand. We get water for the animals from these sloughs. Here, Lizzie, take a bucket and see if you can fill it without..."

Lizzie took the empty bucket from Robert and leaned out with it over the sluggish water. The bucket swung back and forth for a few seconds before she lowered it into the slough. As soon as it filled with water, the bucket sank out of sight, down into the dark water. Lizzie, not expecting the weight of the full bucket, lost her balance and fell into the slough.

"Without falling in," finished Robert. Then he and Seth began laughing at the muddy girl in front of them.

Lizzie looked up at her cousins on the bank, then down at her clothes. Her uniform was covered in mud and green weeds. She was standing over her knees in the slimiest mud she had ever felt.

"Get me out! Just you get me out of here!"

"What happened to you, Lizzie? Did you fall in?" Aunt Kate was busy cleaning the cream separator when Lizzie appeared, dripping and angry, at the screen door. Her aunt paused in the middle of dipping steaming hot water out of the reservoir at the back of the stove. "Don't worry. It used to happen to me. I used to fall in the slough regularly. I was never ready for the weight of a full bucket. Your Uncle Bill laughed himself silly each time."

"Really, Aunt Kate? Did you really make mistakes like me?"

"Oh, all the time. Remember, I came from London just like you. Only I came a long time ago."

AFTER LIZZIE CLEANED up a little, she was ready to start the second part of her special workday.

"Now, remember, cowpats are way worse than sloughs to fall into. So be careful." Seth giggled.

Robert smiled at Lizzie. "Don't mind Seth. He can't help being the way he is. You don't want the green ones. And if they're really soft they're no good either. You just slide this underneath the ones that are firm. Then flip them onto the stoneboat—here, behind old Prince." Robert held out a shovel thing with a wide flat blade.

"But I still don't know what cowpats are. What are they? Why do we want them?"

Robert answered first. "Cowpats are cow manure. They're called pats because...because that's the noise they make hitting the ground. And they're sort of flat, like..." Robert stopped talking. Seth was laughing so much he couldn't say anything at all. Lizzie just stared at the two of them as if they were crazy.

Finally Seth gasped for air and said in a strangled voice, "We used to call them cow *cakes* until Pa told us to stop it because it put him off his food."

"But why would you want to pick up cow manure, anyway? What do you do with it?"

"We burn it. In the stove. That's what's burning in the stove right now."

Robert waited for Seth to stop speaking and then he went on. "We collect them and then we dry them in the soddy beside the house. When the pats are good and dry we bring them in to use as fuel in the stove."

"Not wood? But I thought it was a wood stove." Lizzie had her hands up to her face in horror. "But I thought that was wood smoke coming out of the chimney."

Seth swept his arm around in a circle. "Do you see any wood, Lizzie? Do you ever see us chopping wood? It's one of the chores we don't do. And do you know why? Because there aren't any trees!"

"Yes there are. There are trees over there." Lizzie pointed to the straggly row of trees around the house. "You could use those."

"If we cut down those windbreak trees our house would blow away. Sometimes the wind is so strong you can't stand up in it. It blows away everything that isn't nailed down."

Robert's voice was patient. Lizzie looked at him and smiled a bit. At least he didn't make her feel stupid.

"So, ready or not, Lizzie. Let's get those cowpats." Lizzie made a face.

Robert smiled kindly. "Honest, Lizzie, you'll get used to farm life after a while."

But Lizzie didn't get used to it. She didn't get used to it at all.

Every day she tried to get out of going to the chicken coop or the barn or the pigsty. Sometimes she pretended not to hear when her cousins called her to help. And once or twice she didn't even go inside the coop. She just stood out of sight and pretended. Whenever she returned empty-handed, she would tell her aunt there weren't any eggs.

"That's funny," her aunt would say. "They were laying well yesterday."

When Lizzie got caught out in her stories, she would pout and scrape her foot on the dull plank floor of the kitchen.

LIZZIE'S DAYS WERE long and her nights were lonely.

Lying in bed in the dark one night, Lizzie remembered the days when she wore pretty dresses and had friends over to tea. Now all she had to look forward to was her birthday. In less than a week she would be ten.

"And I'll have a real birthday with a cake and presents. And I can wear a pretty dress," she told herself as she rolled over in her narrow bed and pulled the hand-stitched quilt up to her chin. Dozing, tired out from the hard work of the day, Lizzie dreamed of her special day. Her birthday would be wonderful. Then everything would be all right....

# CHAPTER 4

# It's Not Fair!

"**I** won't! I don't want to! And you can't make me! It's not fair!"

Lizzie dropped the egg basket on the floor. She stuck out her lower lip and stared defiantly at the tall woman in front of her.

"But we need eggs, Lizzie. We need eggs to eat and eggs to sell. You know that. And collecting eggs is your job."

Lizzie said nothing. She was afraid that if she opened her mouth, she would start to cry. Instead, she bit her lip and looked directly at her aunt.

"We also need the milk from the cows and the vegetables from the garden. Lizzie, times are very hard and we must all do our parts."

"I...I don't care. You aren't my mother and you can't make me. It's not fair to make me work today. And...and my name is Elizabeth, not Lizzie!"

Aunt Kate sighed. She put down the basket of washing that she was about to carry outside. Slowly she rubbed the small of her back. Lizzie could see her aunt's rough, red hands. She stared at the woman, wondering how this tired person could be her mother's younger sister.

"Look, Liz...Elizabeth, I know this isn't easy for you, but I can't help what happened to your father and mother. I know that you miss them. So do I. Your mother was my big sister. But you do have to help now that you are with us. We all work together on this farm. We have to or we won't eat."

Aunt Kate sighed again and picked up her basket. She rested it on her hip before speaking. "Now, come on, Lizzie. Pick up the egg basket and see to those eggs. And after that, there are peas to shell and potatoes to lift."

Reluctantly Lizzie picked up the basket and followed her aunt out the creaky screen door. She listened for the *slap* as it closed behind her on the doorframe.

Across the yard was the well, which had a bucket on a pulley where the drinking water came from. Beyond the well stood the chicken coop. Lizzie shuddered. She didn't want to go in it. She didn't want to poke her hand under any more angry hens. And she didn't want to let her cousins see her make mistakes. Or laugh at her voice and her English accent. Even though she'd been on the farm for almost two weeks, she still got things wrong.

"Hurry up, slowpoke!" Seth called to her from the barn. He and Robert were already taking care of the cows. At least that meant the pigs were done and Lizzie wouldn't have to feed them.

But it wasn't fair. Not on this day. Not on her birthday. It wasn't fair to make her fetch eggs on her own birthday!

Trying to pretend that she was somewhere else, Lizzie lifted the latch on the chicken coop and stomped in.

# The Meal

At last it was time for her birthday celebration. Tonight there would be a cake and candles and presents and... Lizzie poured water from the pitcher into the old, chipped basin. She longed for the warm water at home. *That* water came out of a tall tap with a porcelain handle, and it steamed into a china sink. She shivered as she splashed water on her face and bare arms. Cold! And the soap was coarse and stung her nose when she smelt it.

There were so many things to get used to.

The outhouse. Seth snickered when she asked where the water closet was. Even after so many days, Lizzie held her breath whenever she was in or near that awful place. She almost preferred the syrup tin, which sat under her bed in case of emergencies.

Buckets in the kitchen supplied cold water for the house. Precious hot water was heated in a tank behind the stove. This was only used for washing dishes and for baths in a tin tub set in the middle of the kitchen floor. She could have a bath only once a week in the same water that everyone else used. Ugh!

A pitcher and basin in the bedroom instead of a sparkling bathroom with a white sink and a claw-footed tub like the ones at home.

And the stove itself, fueled by dry cowpats! Lizzie wrinkled up her nose at the thought of it. Coal was used only when there was a little extra money. And there was no wood. Apart from those stiff, ugly windbreak trees that stretched out their branches to the sky, there were no trees anywhere.

Lizzie brushed her hair extra hard to remove the ever-present grit and found a ribbon, blue like her eyes. As she tied it, she could hear her mother's soft voice in her head. "Why, Lizzie, you have the bluest eyes of anyone I have

ever seen! You have eyes like my china doll, like the sky, like the sapphire in my ring."

Lizzie stopped tying the bow and thought about her mother. It made her want to cry. But she couldn't. She'd done enough crying to last a lifetime.

"Eyes like my china doll."

Of course that was not the sort of thing that Aunt Kate would say. Aunt Kate was kind but she was strong and silent most of the time. She'd wait so long before answering Lizzie's questions that Lizzie often would forget the question entirely. Lizzie hadn't become used to her aunt's ways yet.

She hadn't become used to anything yet.

LIZZIE WAS TRYING not to think about her birthday as she sat opposite her cousins and played with her food. Miserably she pushed the beans and salt pork around with her fork. She made trails in the sauce with the tines.

Under her lashes she stole glances at the others sitting around the worn, wooden kitchen table.

Not one of them had even wished her "Happy Birthday" when she came down wearing her nicest dress with matching ribbon tied in her hair.

And there was no pile of pretty boxes in the parlor.

Her uncle was eating, bent over his plate like he'd had no food for days. He had dripped brown sauce into his beard. Lizzie tried to look away but the drips fascinated her. She watched as they oozed slowly down the grizzled hair in his beard.

Aunt Kate was eating slowly with that faraway look in her eyes. She ate like she talked. Lizzie wondered what she thought about.

Seth and Robert sat across from Lizzie. Tall and awkward, their faces looked like they'd been cut out of stone. Each one of their hands was as big as both of hers put together. They were nice enough. Even Seth was nice, when he wasn't laughing at her. But if you couldn't talk about cows, there wasn't much to say. And Lizzie couldn't talk about cows to save her life.

Silence. Except for slurping noises that came from her uncle and cousins.

Silence. Except for the ticking of the clock in the corner by the pantry.

Silence. Except for the banging of the screen door in the wind, which had just come up out of nowhere.

Then her uncle cleared his throat. Lizzie jumped.

Uncle Bill said to nobody in particular, "Storm's coming. There'll be a wind before nightfall. Best get out to see to the animals."

Without a word Seth and Robert put down their knives and forks and pushed back their chairs. They grabbed their jackets and headed for the door. Seth picked up the dipper in the bucket and took a quick drink. He sluiced the water round his mouth and threw the remaining contents of the dipper out through the screen door. The wind caught it and blew it back in a fine mist

Aunt Kate awoke from her daydream with a start. She glanced at her husband and then turned to Lizzie.

"Come on, Lizzie. We've got to lock up those hens. We'll have to chase them in early."

Lizzie pouted. She didn't want to go out and chase hens.

She thought about her family, sitting around the dining table at home. There was always chatter. Lizzie talked to her parents and they talked to her. There were smiles and bright lights and music. In her mind she could hear the cheerful clinking of silver spoons against thin china bowls. How could two related families be so different?

Here there was nothing but silence or talk about the cows, the weather or the never-ending hens.

Aunt Kate was waiting by the door. She fidgeted with her jacket and pushed her hair back from her eyes.

"Lizzie, the wind's up. We've got to get those hens in. Got your kerchief?"

"Coming," answered Lizzie unwillingly.

# The Storm

Outside, the sky had darkened.

The few trees around the buildings shook their branches at each other. Lizzie didn't like the trees. They were bleak and frightening. They weren't fun like the trees at home. They weren't waiting to be climbed and explored like the trees in Lizzie's garden. These trees had a job to do. They protected the farmhouse and buildings from the dreadful wind that rolled across the prairie, blowing away the soil and everything else it could get hold of.

The chickens were silly with the wind. They ran this way and that, clucking wildly at each other. The last place they wanted to be was shut up inside the coop.

It took Lizzie and her aunt almost an hour to get the chickens inside. By then the sky had turned black and lightning flashed in the distance.

Lizzie shivered with fear. She hated thunderstorms.

Dust whipped along the ground now, twirling itself into knots around her as she waited for her aunt to fasten the door to the coop. Lizzie's eyes stung and she couldn't see through her tears. Aunt Kate had tightened Lizzie's kerchief in place and it filtered the grit that blew into her face.

It was a struggle to get back to the house. Aunt Kate grabbed hold of the line that was tied between the house and the chicken coop. She called to Lizzie to do the same. With heads bowed, they pushed against the wind, running their hands along the line with each step. There was another line running from the house to the barn. Now

Lizzie knew what they were used for. They were lifelines.

By the time they made it back, the wind was howling round the corners of the buildings. Dust blew up from the ground in dense clouds. Lizzie hung onto the rope as, heads down, they climbed the porch steps.

Once they were inside, Aunt Kate began lighting the paraffin lamps. She kept glancing at the windows, but the dust was so thick, there was nothing to see outside.

"Oh, Lizzie, you've ruined your lovely dress." Aunt Kate patted Lizzie's shoulder absently and stared at the door.

"When will it be over?" asked Lizzie timidly, from her chair by the stove. "When will the noise stop?"

Aunt Kate said nothing, just gazed out the window. Her hands were twisting together. She turned to look at Lizzie as though she hadn't heard a word.

AFTER AN HOUR Aunt Kate's fingers were still working around and through each other. Faster and faster went her fingers. Her eyes looked worried and her lips were tightly pressed together.

At last, turning to face her niece, Aunt Kate said quietly, "Lizzie, I have to go out and find Bill and the boys. They've been gone too long. The livestock must've been hard to move. Sometimes the cows go crazy in the wind."

Lizzie's stomach knotted.

The wind screamed down the chimney.

"You can't leave me here alone! Mother wouldn't want you to!" Lizzie's voice was almost as loud as the wind. "What am I going to do all by myself?"

"Just stay indoors and wait until I get back. You should be safe enough inside."

Terrified, Lizzie begged her aunt to stay. "But what about the storm? And the thunder...and *me*?"

But Aunt Kate had already disappeared into the storm. The door slapped and groaned behind her.

Lizzie could see the dust swirling round inside the house. She covered her ears so she couldn't hear anything. Then she curled up as small as she could and shut her eyes.

# Alone

Lizzie struggled up through layers of sleep.

She could hear her name being called. Over and over it cut through her dream. She could hear her name above the screaming of the wind and the rattling of the doors and windows.

But she didn't want to wake up. Not yet.

She was in the middle of something—something nice—and she wanted to finish it. She wanted to finish her dream.

In her dream, lights and music surrounded Lizzie. On a table were heaps of presents. The boxes were tied with bright ribbons and piled so high that Lizzie couldn't see who was sitting on the other side. She smiled and smiled, and felt that special birthday feeling flow through her body.

"Birthday girl! Birthday girl!"

Lizzie smiled wider and wider until she could feel the skin of her cheeks splitting, revealing another face. The dream Lizzie touched her face with her fingers, and felt fresh, new skin. She turned to see what she looked like in her new birthday face.

"Lizzie...Lizzie...."

Lizzie didn't want to look away from herself. She shrugged and pushed away the voice in her head.

"Lizzie! Help me, Lizzie!"

The words interrupted Lizzie's dream. The spun sugar cake, ribbons, and colored paper all melted away.

Lizzie sat up slowly and rubbed her eyes. She stared around in confusion. The sound of her name played over and over in her ears.

"...Lizzie...Lizzie...."

Lizzie rubbed her eyes again. The grit in them stung and made it hard to focus. She sat up and looked around the silent room.

The lamps were smoking and giving off a strong smell of oil.

The stove was belching black clouds as the wind outside caught the chimney and blew smoke back into the room.

"Aunt Kate? Uncle Bill?" Lizzie's voice came out sad and thin in the silence.

Standing up, Lizzie collected her thoughts.

She couldn't get the feeling out of
her mind that someone needed her.

She looked around the kitchen
and the sitting room but couldn't
find anyone.

The stairway up to the bedrooms
was dark so she found a candle on a
brass stand to carry with her. Slowly
she started up the stairs. The candle
flame threw weird, flickering shadows
against the walls. At the top she
looked around and called, but no
answer came from any of the dark
bedrooms. Lizzie was too frightened
to enter them. Instead she went back
downstairs and into the kitchen.

"Auntie Kate? Auntie Kate? Oh,
where are you, Auntie Kate?"

She looked up at the clock on the
wall. It was almost two hours since
her aunt had left. Outside it looked like
the middle of the night. The sky was
black, and dust covered the storm windows, making it almost impossible to
see out.

Lizzie sat down and began to cry.

# Action

"Lizzie...."

Lizzie jumped up and ran over to the window again. She listened, straining until her ears buzzed with the effort. The door rattled as the wind buffeted it.

Lizzie tried to call out but her voice wouldn't work. "...Who...who...is...it?" She managed to get out a weak question. But the frenzied howling of the wind drowned out any answer.

Then, "...Help...." The word seemed to come in on the wind.

Suddenly she understood. She had to find Aunt Kate!

Lizzie forgot her disappointment that nobody remembered her birthday. She forgot that she hated living on a farm in the middle of the prairie. She forgot that her parents were gone.

Lizzie forgot about everything.

"Aunt Kate! I'm coming, Aunt Kate!" Lizzie pulled on a coat and went to open the door. She fumbled for her kerchief, which was bunched in her pocket, and tied it over her face.

Then she remembered a story that her aunt had once told her.

The story was about a little girl who had gone out onto the prairie to rescue her cat during a windstorm. The little girl opened the door and slipped out when nobody was looking. The family hadn't realized she was missing until her mother went into the little girl's room to say goodnight. The family didn't find the little girl until the next day when the wind dropped. She was out on the prairie, covered in dust, grit, and sand. She'd gone out with nothing to help her find her way back home, and she'd just kept on wandering out into the empty prairie, miles away from her house.

Lizzie shuddered as she remembered that story. She'd been too scared to ask her aunt if the little girl was still alive when her parents found her.

Lizzie looked for something that would show her the way back. Something she could tie to the back door handle and hold onto while she went out looking for her aunt.

She found an old clothesline tucked away inside a drawer. Lizzie grabbed the clothesline and went to the door. It took all her strength to push against the wind. When she did open the door, it slammed back against the outside wall of the house. The wind rushed in, scattering papers and sand about the room. Carefully Lizzie tied the line to the door handle.

One knot. Two knots. Three knots.

Then she set off in the direction of the chicken coop.

# CHAPTER 9

# The Search

Lizzie stumbled on—head down, hand over her eyes—toward the coop. She could hardly see in front of her face. She dared not lift her head. She was afraid that the wind would throw something right into her face.

As she struggled forward, she said over and over, "I'm coming. I'm coming. Don't worry, I'm coming." It made her steps easier when she said the words aloud. It gave her a rhythm to move to.

Just as she got up close to the chicken coop, she stumbled over something embedded in the ground. As she tried to get by it, she realized what it was—a huge branch from one of the guard trees.

Carefully Lizzie stepped around it. She lifted the clothesline up to clear it.

Then Lizzie heard the voice again. This time it came from quite close. Lizzie could hear it over the roar of the wind. "…Lizzie…help me…Lizzie…."

"Aunt Kate! Where are you?"

"Lizzie…my leg…I've hurt my leg…."

The voice was faint but close. She could hear it quite clearly now. It came from somewhere out beyond the coop—out past the machine shed, which was just behind the chicken coop.

Lizzie hung tightly onto her lifeline. She edged away from the corner of the coop and kept on going, one foot sliding in front of the other.

Although the wind grabbed and tugged at the line in her fingers, Lizzie would not let go. She would not get lost like that poor little girl who had wandered out onto the prairie. She would not let Aunt Kate lie out there alone, covered in dust.

Lizzie lost her bearings as she went beyond the corner of the coop. She rarely went out this far on the farm. Even in good weather she didn't like the emptiness of the flat land that stretched out to meet the horizon. Now Lizzie felt she had stepped into space.

But a faint noise over her left shoulder told her which way to turn.

She shuffled carefully past another branch and some metal roofing lying on the ground. The roofing frightened her.

It banged and clanged like some wild, metallic creature. It seemed ready to lift off the ground and run her down. The branches were bad enough, but a sheet of heavy metal flying through the air was much worse.

Gingerly, Lizzie slid her feet past the roofing and went on her way.

The voice was getting a little louder. It sounded muffled, as if it were under a pile of sheets. But it was definitely closer now.

"Auntie Kate! Auntie Kate! Where are you? I'm coming as fast as I can."

A sound like a sob came from almost under Lizzie's right foot and stopped her in mid-stride. She gasped as the sob came again.

Her aunt was right at her feet. Lizzie couldn't see her at all.

Making sure the clothesline was securely wound around her fingers, Lizzie knelt down and felt around with her free hand. She came upon something sharp that hurt. She could feel it slice into her finger. It had to be glass.

Lizzie imagined her aunt under a pile of broken glass. The machine shed had a window. She remembered it now—a large pane of dusty glass set into a scabbed and peeling frame.

Quickly Lizzie pulled her hand back and stood up again. It made her dizzy to stand up against the wind. Instead of feeling with her hand, she pushed her toe forward.

The sob came again. This time Lizzie felt a softer obstruction in front of her. She knelt down a second time and ran her hand gently over the bundle in front of her. It

moaned and a sticky substance came off on Lizzie's hand.

Aunt Kate.

Carefully Lizzie tied the line around her waist. With both hands free now, she found her aunt's head and stroked her cheek.

"It's me, Aunt Kate. It's Lizzie. I've come to get you. I've got a line tied from me to the door so we won't get lost. Can you walk at all?"

Aunt Kate groaned and tried to say something. But the only other sound she made was a weak cry.

Lizzie sat down beside her aunt. She stroked the older woman's hair. Then she tried to think of some way of getting them back to the house.

# CHAPTER 10

# The Rescue

The wind howled. Adding to the noise was the sound of objects crashing to the ground.

Lizzie had an image of metal roofing snaking through the air straight at them. She shivered. She had to think of something quickly.

A louder crash came from much closer. Lizzie jerked her head up and stared into the thick blackness. She strained to see what was happening but couldn't make out anything. More and more loud bangs came. Then a huge mass rushed by her. It clanged and bounced off the ground, twanging as it went.

Metal!

The granary!

The metal must be coming off the granary!

Lizzie was terrified. This meant that the pieces would be huge, curved sheets of tin with edges like knives. Uncle Bill had warned her about this building. He had told her to stay clear away from it in a windstorm.

At the memory of her uncle's words, Lizzie almost jumped up and raced away in the direction of the house.

But she didn't.

She swallowed her fear and crouched beside her aunt, waiting for the thudding of her heart to slow.

Gently Lizzie tugged on the lifeline. She could feel it tight at her waist. It made her feel better. She would not end up out on the prairie in a windstorm with her injured aunt.

Lizzie tugged again. And then again.

Something was wrong.

She could feel the line but it was jammed. It wouldn't move at all. Whatever had been blown down had pinned the clothesline beneath its weight.

Lizzie tugged again but carefully. She didn't want to break the old line.

Beside her, Aunt Kate moaned and moved slightly. She shifted a little more, then cried out in pain.

"Don't move, Aunt Kate. We have to try to get back to the house. But the line is stuck and I don't want to break it."

Lizzie wriggled her way around her aunt's crumpled body and felt along the line. It was buried under something. There seemed to be enough slack in the rope to move a bit farther, but not much. Lizzie could feel it tighten. She had to free the clothesline. She had to get it loose without breaking it. Lizzie returned to her aunt and lay down very close to her. She said right into Aunt Kate's ear, "The rope is jammed. I'm going to try to work it free. Then we can get back to the house. I won't be long."

Lizzie ducked her head and stumbled away from her aunt. She ran her hand along the rope until she could feel it dip down toward the ground. With trembling hands Lizzie felt along the taut line until she came to a hard mass.

Another heavy branch.

Lizzie strained her weight against the branch until she thought her arms would break.

Nothing. The branch didn't move.

She tried again. Gathering her strength, she crouched down and pushed up from the knees.

The branch gave a little.

Lizzie pushed again, and the branch suddenly rolled forward. Lizzie fell on top of it. The clothesline sprang free!

She turned around to find her aunt.

But now she was confused. She could find her way back to the house with the rope, but could she find her way back to her aunt? She hadn't thought about that before.

"Aunt Kate! Say something, Aunt Kate! I have to find you again!"

Her aunt called out weakly. Lizzie turned and, following the faint cries, slowly retraced her steps back past the coop to the shed.

The wind whistled around her ears and kicked up dust devils, but Lizzie pressed on until she could feel her aunt's body with her toe.

"Don't worry. I'm back. Now all we have to do is follow the line to the house."

Lizzie's shoulder ached from pushing the branch off the line and Aunt Kate was heavy. She pulled her aunt to her feet, but Aunt Kate's knee was badly hurt and she had to lean on Lizzie.

Very slowly the two set out to find the house. The life-line was tied tightly to Lizzie's waist but she had to hold it carefully, winding it up as they got closer to the door handle.

It was awkward holding onto the loose loops of line and to her aunt at the same time. Lizzie's arms began to tremble with the strain.

"Not too far, Aunt Kate. We aren't too far away now."

It seemed to take a lifetime to get to the porch. At almost each step, Aunt Kate called out in pain. But they kept moving. Even when the line jammed again—and Lizzie had to flick it a few times to loosen it—they kept going on toward the house.

Lizzie's lungs hurt with the effort, and with the dust. Her heart pounded in her chest like a hammer. By the time she got her aunt to the bottom of the steps, Lizzie could do nothing more. All she could do was sit beside her injured aunt and wait to be found.

# A Family Together

Afterward, Lizzie could remember almost nothing of the journey back to the house. All she could really remember was the sound of Seth's voice coming out of the darkness and Robert's strong arms lifting her up. She called out in panic at leaving her aunt's side.

"Hush, Lizzie. We've got her safe." Uncle Bill's voice sounded concerned as he spoke over the moaning of the wind.

And then silence. The door opened and closed on the storm, and she was inside.

Safe.

The stove was relit and the oil lamps trimmed. The kitchen was warm and seemed full of people. Concerned faces came into view and then disappeared.

A blanket was tucked around her. Lizzie closed her eyes and slept.

"WHAT I DON'T understand is how Lizzie could hear me all the way back to the house here. I just don't know how she could make out anything in that storm."

Aunt Kate was sitting propped up in bed. Her foot was on a pillow. She looked uncomfortable to be sitting in bed in the middle of the day. The doctor had told her she was lucky not to have a broken leg rather than a badly wrenched knee and a twisted ankle. Uncle Bill sat beside the bed. Seth and Robert leaned self-consciously against the far wall.

They all turned to look at Lizzie as her aunt mused out loud again. "I just cannot work that out."

Lizzie couldn't answer. She could only remember waking up to the sound of her aunt's voice. The rest of that dreadful evening was a blur.

Uncle Bill opened his mouth. He hesitated.

He cleared his throat and tried again. "No telling what would have happened to your Aunt Kate if you hadn't gone out looking for her, Lizzie. We had such a hard time with those cows, all running around in circles crazy-like."

He closed his mouth and wiped at his face. Then he raised his head and continued. "Good thing you tied that clothesline on the door handle. If you hadn't, no telling where you'd have got to. As it was, we had to follow the fences out to the pasture. It was so dark we couldn't see a dang thing."

Both cousins nodded silently. They shuffled their feet and coughed a few times. Even Seth didn't speak.

"Come here, Lizzie." Aunt Kate held her arms out to her niece. "Come and let me give you a hug."

Lizzie went over to the bed.

"Sorry we forgot all about your birthday. It's so hard sometimes," her voice trailed away. Then she continued, her voice firm, "but that's no excuse for forgetting. We'll make it up to you as soon as I can move around again. We'll have a cake. And...and a party."

She smiled at her niece.

"Lizzie, I know this is nothing like the life you're used to. And it's sometimes hard for us to forget our work long enough to remember how lonely you must be. But we really love you. I am so sorry about your parents, but you are part of our family now and we'll try to make you feel welcome.

Seth and Robert both nodded at their mother's words. A shy grin creased Seth's face.

He shifted off the wall and went to stand beside his

mother. "We've got a birthday present for you, Lizzie. We've got a pony for you. Something to ride back and forth to school. We're going to get it tomorrow. Do you want to come with us to pick it up?"

Lizzie nodded, speechless. She tried to hide her tears, but they escaped and ran down her cheeks. She wasn't used to being an orphan yet and she wasn't used to her relatives' ways. But she knew they loved her

And that made a difference.

THAT NIGHT, TUCKED up in her bed with no wind howling, just the whisper of the prairie breeze through the grasses, Lizzie thought about her Aunt Kate. She thought about Uncle Bill, Seth, and Robert. She thought about the hens and the pigs. She thought about the old table downstairs and the warmth of the kitchen.

She thought about the pony waiting for her.

And as she drifted off to sleep, Lizzie smiled.

**Coal**—A fuel made from a hard substance found in the earth. Coal fuel heated homes before oil, electricity, or gas.

**Cowpats, or pats**—Cow manure.

**Dipper**—A long-handled pot used to scoop water out of a bucket

**Dray**—A workhorse; a horse that pulls wagons or carts; also, the name given to the wagon itself.

**Dust devil**—A small whirlwind that stirs up dust in a column.

**Dust storm**—Sand, grit or soil picked up by the wind and blown away. Very common on the prairie during the 1930's, dust storms could be so dense that people could not see their way even in their own yards.

**Granary**—A building where grain is stored.

**Gumbo**—Very sticky and slippery mud, which occurs when the soil contains a large amount of very fine dust.

**Homestead**—The land, house and other farm buildings; also, to settle on a section of land given by the government in exchange for the promise to clear and plant the property.

**Homesteader**—The person who settles on and farms the land given to him or her by the government. Also known as a **sod-buster**.

**Kerchief**—A square of cloth tied around the neck or over the head. During dust storms a kerchief protected the wearer from breathing in large amounts of dust.

**Lifeline**—A rope or cord tied from one building to another. During dust storms or blizzards, homesteaders used lifelines to find their way from one building to another.

# GLOSSARY

**Lift**—To "lift" potatoes means to dig them out of the ground.

**Manger**—A box or trough used to feed cows, horses, sheep, etc. Mangers were often made with slatted sides so animals could eat but not climb in and spoil the feed.

**Outhouse**—A small, outdoor toilet; usually a hole dug in the ground with a cutout wooden seat and surrounded by walls and a roof.

**Pantry**—A small, cool room used for storing food.

**Paraffin**—Flammable white oil used as fuel for lamps and for making candles.

**Parlor**—A formal living room that was rarely used except to entertain special visitors.

**Pigsty**—A small fenced area for pigs usually containing a small covered shelter.

**Prairie**—An area of grassy, flat land with few trees. Most of central North America is prairie.

**Reservoir**—a container built into the back of a stove where water could be heated.

**Ruts**—Grooves and ridges made on dirt roads, which harden in the sun.

**Separator**—a hand-operated machine that separates cream from milk

**Sod**—a piece of ground with the grass and its roots still in it.

**Sod-buster**—Someone who breaks up the land on their homestead in order to farm it. Also known as a **homesteader**.

**Soddy**—A house dug out of the ground with a sod roof and sometimes sod walls as well.

**Slop**—water or milk mixed with

kitchen waste and fed to pigs; also, to feed the pigs.

**Slough**—side channel of a stream often dug for irrigation.

**Stoneboat**—A low sled with logs for runners used to carry stones from fields and other heavy loads.

**Trim**—To adjust the height of the wick in an oil lamp, either to stop it smoking or to increase the brightness.

**Water closet**—indoor room with a flushing toilet.

**Windbreak**—A line of trees or shrubs that acts as a screen to protect buildings from the wind. The roots of the windbreak also help keep the soil from blowing away.

# SUGGESTED READING

## FOR YOUNG READERS

Bannatyne-Cugnet, Jo and Moore, Yvette. *A Prairie Year*. Montreal, Tundra Books, 1994.

Coombs, Karen Mueller. *Children of the Dust Days (Picture the American Past)*. Minneapolis, Carolrhoda Books, 2003.

Kurelek, William and Englehart, Margaret S. *They Sought a New World: The Story of European Immigration to North America.* Montreal, Tundra Books, 1985.

Meltzer, Milton. *Driven from the Land: The Story of the Dust Bowl* (Great Journeys). New York, Benchmark Books, 2000.

Stein, R. Conrad. *The Great Depression (Cornerstones of Freedom)*. Chicago, Children's Press, 1993.

# INDEX

# INDEX

# BIOGRAPHY

SALLY FITZ-GIBBON was born in England but came to Canada with her family when she was a year old. She grew up in North Vancouver, British Columbia and attended The University of British Columbia. Sally decided early on that she wanted to write, but she got sidetracked by a horse and moved to a farm instead. There she raised her two children along with numerous horses, sheep, cattle, chickens, pigs, rabbits, guinea pigs, dogs, and cats. Sally is the author of *The Patchwork House* and *Two Shoes, Blue Shoes, New Shoes*. Her interest in the history of homesteaders and the hardships they endured led to this, her third book for children. Sally now lives on an island not far from Vancouver in a house overlooking the sea, which she shares with her husband, two dogs and an ancient ex-barn cat.

# B I O G R A P H Y

MURIEL WOOD was born in Kent, England. She obtained her diploma in design and painting at the Canterbury College of Art before immigrating to Canada. Since the early 1960's her artwork has appeared in many places: magazines, books, stamps, porcelains, and posters. In addition, she has displayed her paintings in a number of group and one-woman shows. Her children's books include L.M. Montgomery's *Anne of Green Gables*, Margaret Laurence's *The Olden Day's Coat,* and *Apples and Angel Ladders* and *Old Bird* by Irene Morck. A former instructor at the Ontario College of Art and Design in Toronto, Muriel now draws and paints full time. She lives with her husband and two cats in Port Hope, Ontario.